Ten Little Bunnies

by Robin Spowart

Cartwheel
·B·O·O·K·S·®

SCHOLASTIC INC.

New York   Toronto   London   Auckland   Sydney   Mexico City   New Delhi   Hong Kong

One little bunny
drumming...

Two little bunnies
flying...

Zoom!

Zoom!

Three little bunnies
giggling . . .

Hee!

Hee!

Four little bunnies
helping Daddy.

Five little bunnies
singing...

La!
La!

Six little bunnies
hugging Mama.

Seven little bunnies
sliding…

Yippee!

Eight little bunnies
eating...

Yummy!

Nine little bunnies

swinging so high.

Ten little bunnies waving...